## About This Book

Believe it or not, once upon a time, James and I were both kids.
Life was much easier in those days because there were rules most people
followed. Holding the door for someone. A nod and a hello.
Even just saying "please." Most kids did those things back then,
but now there is confusion in many places.
James and I believe we can bring that civility and compassion back into the
world. Let's start today with our children, by encouraging them to always say
that wonderful, magical word: *please.*

—Bill O'Reilly

BILL O'REILLY &
JAMES PATTERSON

GIVE PLEASE A CHANCE

# Can I keep him?

Illustrated by Scott Magoon

Please?

# Can I lick the bowl?

Illustrated by Tracy Dockray

Please?

# Daddy, make the splinter go away.

Illustrated by Kate Babok

Please?

# Can I have seconds?

Illustrated by Ziyue Chen

Please?

I need a friend.

Illustrated by Joe Sutphin

Please?

# Zip me up!

Illustrated by Frank Morrison

Please?

It's so hot out!

Illustrated by Ziyue Chen

Please?

# Am I clean yet?

Illustrated by Daniel Roode

Please?

It's my favorite book. Ever!

Illustrated by Olga and Aleksey Ivanov

Please?

I am *too* big enough.

Illustrated by Alina Chau

Please?

# Which part goes where?

Illustrated by Amy June Bates

Please?

# Help! I'm stuck!

Illustrated by John Nez

Please?

# Can we take them all?

Illustrated by Julie Robine

Please?

# I really, really, really need a cookie!

Illustrated by Donald Wu

Please?

# I can do that too!

Illustrated by Jennifer Zivoin

Please?

# Trick and treat?

Illustrated by Begona Corbalan

Please?

# Again! Again!

Illustrated by Ruth Galloway

Please?

# Dear God, can you hear me?
# I'm little.

～

Illustrated by Amy Bates

Please?

# Swing me!

Illustrated by Tracy Dockray

Please?

I've been *extra* good this year.

Illustrated by Scott Magoon

Please?

# Can I get a hug?

Illustrated by Ruth Galloway

Please?

1 3 5 7 9 10 8 6 4 2

Young Arrow
20 Vauxhall Bridge Road
London SW1V 2SA

Young Arrow is part of the Penguin Random House group of companies whose addresses can be found at
global.penguinrandomhouse.com.

Copyright © 2016 by William O'Reilly and James Patterson

William O'Reilly and James Patterson have asserted their right to be identified as the authors of this Work
in accordance with the Copyright, Designs and Patents Act 1988.

First published by Young Arrow in 2016

www.penguin.co.uk

A CIP catalogue record for this book is available from the British Library.

ISBN 9781784756802